KU-002-978

Now I am a Pirate

Now I am a Pirate

Catherine Osborne
photography by Christina Wilson
illustrations by Aaron Blecha
styling and projects by
Rose Hammick

RYLAND
PETERS
& SMALL

LONDON NEW YORK

Designer Carl Hodson
Senior editor Catherine Osborne
Picture research Emily Westlake
Production manager Patricia Harrington
Publishing director Alison Starling
Art director Leslie Harrington

Pirate cooking recipes adapted from
recipes by **Caroline Marson**.

First published in the United Kingdom
in 2008 by Ryland Peters & Small
20–21 Jockey's Fields
London WC1R 4BW

First published in the United States
in 2008 by Ryland Peters & Small Inc.
519 Broadway, 5th Floor
New York, NY 10012
www.rylandpeters.com

10 9 8 7 6 5 4 3 2 1

Text, design, illustrations and photographs
© Ryland Peters & Small 2008.

All rights reserved. No part of this
publication may be reproduced, stored
in a retrieval system, or transmitted in
any form or by any means, electronic,
mechanical, photocopying or otherwise,
without the prior permission of
the publisher.

ISBN: 978-1-84597-743-6

Printed in China

A CIP record for this book is available
from the British Library.

**NOTE: All projects and recipes will
require an adult's help.**

This book
belongs to

A picture of me as a pirate

stick photo or
drawing here

famous pirates

There are many famous pirates, but the ones who have everyone quaking in their boots are Captain Hook, Long John Silver and Blackbeard.

Captain Hook

'TICK TOCK, TICK TOCK'. Have you ever heard about the pirate, the croc and the clock? Captain Hook is a ruthless pirate captain and enemy of the notorious Peter Pan and his friends The Lost Boys. Hook's hand was cut off by Peter during a fight and fed to a croc – who found it quite yummy. Hoping to get another cheeky bite of Hook, the croc follows him wherever he goes. Fortunately for Hook and his crew, the croc's presence is always betrayed by the 'tick tock' of his belly from a clock he once swallowed. Hook and his dastardly right-hand man Smee would love to get their revenge on Peter Pan and make him walk the plank. If only they had the brains – Peter Pan and The Lost Boys are far too cunning to fall into the traps they set (much to Hook's annoyance).

Long John Silver

'SHIVER ME TIMBERS!' If you ever hear these words uttered, you'll more than likely find yourself face to face with the infamous Long John Silver. He's a bit of a tough old pirate, and is known for his wooden leg and his parrot Captain Flint. He's wanted for stealing treasure from his shipmates Jim Hawkins, Ben Gunn and Doctor Lively, so listen out for the tap, tap of his wooden leg!

Blackbeard

THE BEARD IS TO BE FEARED!
Blackbeard is the most ruthless pirate known to have sailed the high seas. He prevailed by fear alone, and legend states that he even used to light matches woven into his beard during battle. Can you imagine that?

11

You will need:
1 sheet cream
A3/ledger card,
a sponge, brown
and black acrylic
or poster paint, a
small paintbrush,
coloured felt-tip
pens/markers,
a length of red
ribbon (approx
40 cm/16 in).

Making a pirate map

1) **Make the shape.** Roughly tear the corners off the cream card and tear the edges to make it look worn. Run water over the card and while the paper is very wet sponge on the brown paint.

2) **Paint.** Dip the brush into the black paint and paint around the torn edges, so it looks like the paper has been burnt. Using felt tip pens/markers that smudge when used with water, draw your treasure map. Make lots of smudges to make the map look older.

3) **Roll the scroll.** When the map is dry, roll it up and tie the red ribbon around it to form a scroll.

pirate
wardrobe

Ahoy m'hearties! To participate in true pirate skulduggery, you need to look the part.

You'll never become one of the motley crew if you turn up on the poop deck in your best clothes. Pirates like to look scruffy, so find your striped top with holes in, torn trousers, worn waistcoat, scuffed boots and skull and crossbone headscarf. Higher-ranking pirates wear a hat, and some even have a wooden leg, eye patch or a hook for a hand – marks of swashbuckling sword fights lost and won. An older pirate bears many battle scars, and shows them off to scare his enemies and impress his crew. No pirate's wardrobe is complete without a trusty parrot. Perched on your shoulder, he can whisper news to you, especially if it involves mutiny. The last thing you want on your hands is a ship of mad mutineers!

You will need:
1 sheet white
A3/ledger paper,
a pencil, scissors,
2 sheets black
A3/ledger card,
clear glue and glue
brush, black elastic,
a couple of sheets
of coloured paper
of your choice for
the pirate shapes.

Making a pirate hat

1

2

1) **Creating shapes.** Fold the sheet of white paper in half. Draw half a hill shape on one side of the folded paper and cut out. Unfold the shape and trace around it with a pencil onto the black card. Draw an eye patch on the leftover card. Cut a strip from the second sheet of card, slightly longer than the diameter of your head (use 2 strips if required). Bend it into a circle and glue the ends together.

2) **Finishing touches.** Cut out the hill shape and the eye patch from the black card. Cut halfway into the eye patch and overlap the sides along the cut, making a shallow cone. Secure with glue. Pierce two holes at the top right- and left-hand corners of the patch with a pair of scissors. Get an adult to help. Thread the elastic through the holes, adjust to fit your head and tie. Decorate the hat with cut-out pirate shapes, such as a sword and skull and crossbone. Glue the hat to the band.

19

pirate ways

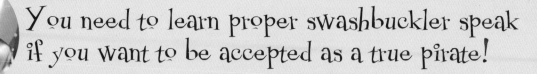

You need to learn proper swashbuckler speak if you want to be accepted as a true pirate!

Shiver me timbers: an expression of shock, surprise or annoyance.

Ahoy me hearties: a form of greeting – 'Hello my friends!'

Yo-ho-ho: pirate laughter.

Matey: a shipmate or friend.

Pieces of eight: silver coins.

Doubloons: gold coins.

Anchor's aweigh!: yelled out when pulling the anchor up.

Land ahoy!: shouted when you finally spot land after months of just seeing sea.

Avast!: stop!

Aye: yes.

Booty: treasure.

Davy Jones' locker: the bottom of the sea, where the souls of dead men lie.

Grog: a pirate's favourite drink.

Lily-livered: cowardly.

Scurvy dog: an insult.

Ooooh arhhh: an expression of surprise or agreement.

Landlubber: a person who doesn't know a thing about seamanship. They'd never make a good pirate!

Stern: the back of the ship.

Bow: the front of the ship.

Starboard: the right-hand side of the ship.

Port: the left-hand side of the ship.

Now that you've got the lingo, it's time to start some pirate mischief...

Pirates are known for getting into trouble. They like to raid ships and rob them of their booty, and love to make enemy pirates walk the plank. Make sure you're not the one who gets fed to the sharks by brushing up on your pirating skills, from sword-fighting and climbing the rigging to navigating using the stars and learning how to read treasure maps.

Although pirates like to get up to no good, there is great camaraderie on board ship, and there's nothing they like more than singing a good old sea shanty. They may scare away the seagulls with their loud and hearty voices, but it raises the spirits, particularly if they've just sailed through a dangerous storm. So, it's 'Ahoy m'hearties!' and 'Way hay and up she rises!'

You will need:
4–5 sheets white card, scissors, a pencil, coloured paper (enough for number of shapes required), coloured A3/ledger card (enough for number of flags required) clear glue and glue brush, string.

1) Make the templates. Cut 4 different pirate shapes out of the white card. Use these as templates. Trace around them onto the coloured paper until you have the number of shapes you require. You need two shapes for each flag. Cut out.

2) Make the flags. Cut long rectangular strips from the coloured card, fold them in half and cut out a 'V' shape from each unfolded end. Stick a shape onto both sides of the folded flag. Make sure you don't stick them upside down!

3) Hang them up. Fold the flags over a length of string. Hang them around your bedroom or use them as party decorations. Ask an adult to help. Make as many as you require to decorate your pirate's cabin.

26

Making pirate flags

pirates aboard

Shipshape

Everything above deck on a pirate ship is kept tidy, so clumsy pirates don't trip and fall overboard. Ropes are kept neatly coiled, the deck is regularly scrubbed by the cabin boy and sails are patched up and rolled ready for use. Below deck it's a different story. A pirate's living quarters are a mess and very stinky, because they don't care about cleaning. They leave half-eaten food everywhere, never put their clothes away and rarely make their hammocks. And let's not forget the rats. They thrive on the leftovers dropped on the floor by lazy pirates with bad table manners. A pirate wouldn't be surprised to wake up to a rat gnawing on his cheesy toe. Gross!

You will need:
2 cardboard
tubes, brown
acrylic or poster
paint, PVA/white
glue, scissors,
sticky/Scotch tape,
red string, 1 sheet
of gold shiny card,
6–8 adhesive gems.

Making a pirate telescope

1) Paint and cut the tubes. Give 2 cardboard tubes 2 coats of paint. Acrylic paint covers best, but you can also use poster paint. Add a tablespoon of PVA/white glue to the paint. This will give the telescope a sheen. Wait for the paint to dry and then cut along the length of one tube.

2) Roll and tie. Roll the cut tube so that it is slightly smaller than the uncut tube. Tape it back together, making sure it fits snugly into the uncut tube but also has room to move. Punch two tiny holes either side of the taped tube at one end with a pair of scissors. Ask an adult for help. Thread two lengths of string (each just short of the length of the tube) through the holes and tie. Feed the small tube (non-string end first) into the large tube until it extends out the other side.

3) String it together. The two lengths of string should extend along the interior of the large tube. Tape the ends of the string to the bottom (inside) of the large tube to keep the small tube in place.

4) Final touches. Decorate with strips of shiny card and gems.

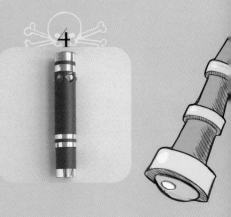

33

pirates at play

When they're not causing havoc or manning the sails during rough seas, pirates like to have fun.

If there's one thing a pirate loves, it's proving his or her bravery. What better way to do this than to have a rigging race? For the lily-livered who are scared of heights this certainly isn't a game for you! It not only requires nerves of steel, but also great agility. The one who makes it to the crow's nest first is rewarded with a big tankard of pirate punch. NOTE: Pirate punch can make you hiccup a lot, so make sure you don't drink too much of it!

For a real show of strength, pirates will grab a coil of old ship rope and start a tug of war. Teams are divided according to head attire – so hats against head scarves! Sometimes, to give everyone a bit of a laugh, one team will let go of the rope so that the other team all fall flat on their pirate pants. If you decide to do this, just make sure there's no one bigger and stronger than you on the other team. The last thing you want is a big angry pirate challenging you to a duel.

'On your marks, get set, go!'
There are even games for pirates who have been injured in battles.

The Peg Leg Race is the most fun. Pirates with wooden legs race each other from the stern (back) to the bow (front) of the ship. The pirate who reaches the bow first wins. The one who loses is thrown overboard, and rescued once he's had a bit of swim.

39

pirate grub

'Water, water everywhere and not a drop to drink!' Pirates can be at sea for months without a hint of land in sight. During these trying times they often run short of food and water. It's therefore important for pirates to stock up on goods whenever they are ashore. Sometimes things get so desperate they end up eating the little grubs that live in their biscuits! YUCK! The following pages contain some favourite pirate munchies.

42

Looted-up Pita Pockets

Fill 'em up and pack 'em in! Well-fed pirates are happy pirates, so loosen your swashbuckling belts and make room for these bountiful booties.

Both recipes fill 6–8 halves of pita bread

Tuna and carrot salad:

Combine a drained 185 g/small can of tuna with 2 coarsely grated carrots, 2 tablespoons chopped flat leaf parsley and 2 tablespoons mayonnaise in a small bowl.

Cheese, bacon and tomato:

Combine 50 g/½ cup coarsely grated cheddar cheese with 2 tablespoons crème fraîche/mayonnaise, 2 chopped tomatoes and 4 strips of crispy bacon, finely chopped.

Jolly Roger Fruity Boats

Keep the scabby scurvy at bay with these fruity treats.

3 large oranges
1 packet fruit-flavoured jelly/jello
cocktail sticks/toothpicks
rice paper or coloured paper cut
   into sail shapes

Makes 12 boats

Method

1. Ask an adult to cut the oranges in half. Squeeze out the juice, taking care not to pierce the skins, and scrape out the insides of the oranges. Make up the jelly/jello according to the packet instructions (with a little less water so that they set well). Put the orange shells on a baking sheet and pour in the jelly/jello mixture, making sure they are full to the top and the surface is level. Refrigerate until set.

2. Once set, ask an adult to cut the oranges into wedges, using a sharp, wet knife. Pierce the paper sails with a cocktail stick/toothpick and attach a sail to each fruity boat.

Bone Crunching Skull and Crossbone Gingerbreads

Get your pirate gnashers around these tasty morsels. They're much tastier than grubs and far less chewy. Save some crumbs for the rats!

Makes 25 cookies

225 g/1⅔ cups plain/all-purpose
flour, plus extra for dusting
1 teaspoon ground ginger
1 teaspoon ground cinnamon
1 teaspoon bicarbonate of
soda/baking soda
60 g/½ stick butter
2 tablespoons unrefined
dark brown sugar
80 g/¼ cup golden/corn syrup
1 tablespoon beaten egg
icing/confectioners' sugar and
2 tubes of ready-to-use
coloured icing to decorate

Method

1. Ask an adult to preheat the oven to 190°C (375°F) Gas 5. Cover two baking sheets with greaseproof paper/grease two cookie sheets.
2. Ask an adult to blend the flour, ginger, cinnamon and bicarbonate of soda/baking soda in a food processor. Add the butter and whizz until the mixture resembles fine breadcrumbs. Add the sugar, syrup and egg and blend to form a soft dough.
3. Roll out the dough to 5 mm/¼ inch thickness. Using skull and crossbone cookie cutters, cut out and put them on the baking/cookie sheets. Ask an adult to help you put them in the oven. Bake for 8–10 minutes until golden brown. Ask an adult to remove them from the oven. Leave until firm, then transfer to a wire rack to cool.
4. To decorate, dust with icing/confectioners' sugar and gently squeeze out the coloured icing from the tubes to draw the eyes and mouth.

45

Treasure Island Punch

This energy juice will go down quicker than your parrot can say 'pieces of eight'.

175 g/6 oz. sugar cubes
175 ml/¾ cup boiling water
200 g/7 oz. ripe melon or mango, peeled,
    deseeded/seeded and chopped
freshly squeezed juice of 2 limes and 2 lemons
500 ml/2 cups chilled pineapple or orange juice
500 ml/2 cups sparkling mineral water
ice cubes, to serve

Method

1. Ask an adult to help you stir the sugar and water together in a pan until the sugar has dissolved. Set aside to cool.
2. Blend the melon in a blender until smooth. Pour into a jug/pitcher with the sugar syrup and lime and lemon juices. Stir in the pineapple juice and chill.
3. Top with mineral water and serve in glasses half-filled with ice cubes.

This is to certify that

....

has now officially become
a pirate of the worst kind

Picture credits and stockists

Picture credits and UK stockists

Photography by Christina Wilson, illustrations by Aaron Blecha

Key: a=above, b=below, r=right, l=left, c=centre.

Boden
08456775000
www.boden.co.uk
Page 4: skull and crossbone top from Boden; Page 24r: skull and crossbone top.

CB Partystore
www.cbparty.co.uk
Page 43b pirate balloons.

The Conran Shop
Page 48: map.

DZD
+44 (0)20 7388 7488
www.dzd.co.uk/
Page 2bc: skull garland; Page 24r: ship's wheel & parrot; Page 36: ship's wheel, anchor, flag & skeleton; Page 38al: parrot & ship's wheel.

Early Learning Center
www.elc.co.uk
Pages 30b & 31ar: pirate figures & pirate ship.

Hope and Greenwood
+44 (0)20 7613177
www.hopeandgreenwood.co.uk
Page 2al: sweets.

Ikea
www.ikea.com
Page 35: treasure chest.

Maggie Bulman Costumes
+44 (0)20 8693 9733
www.enchantedcastle.co.uk
Page 21: boy's costume on left; Page 23l & br: costume; Page 38al: flag.

Olive Loves Alfie
+44 (0)20 7241 4212
www.olivelovesalfie.co.uk
Page 45: skull & crossbone cookie cutters.

Paperchase
www.paperchase.co.uk

Pedlars
+44 (0)1330 850400
www.pedlars.co.uk
Page 29 & 31br: flag.

US stockists

JoAnn Fabrics
Locations nationwide
Visit www.joann.com for details of your nearest store.

Just Kid Costumes
1-888-821-4890
www.justkidcostumes.com

Pottery Barn Kids
www.potterybarnkids.com

Thank you to our special pirate models: Arthur, Ashley, Blaise, Cameron, Lauren, Leo, Ollie, Shayan and Dolly the ship's dog.